THE MUSICAL OF MUSICALS
THE MUSICAL!

Music by
Eric Rockwell

Lyrics by
Joanne Bogart

Book by
Eric Rockwell and Joanne Bogart

A SAMUEL FRENCH ACTING EDITION

SAMUEL FRENCH
FOUNDED 1830

NEW YORK HOLLYWOOD LONDON TORONTO

SAMUELFRENCH.COM

ISBN 978-0-573-63312-6   Printed in U.S.A.   #15752

RENTAL MATERIALS

An orchestration consisting of 4 Piano/Vocal Scores will be loaned two months prior to the production ONLY on the receipt of the Licensing Fee quoted for all performances, the rental fee and a refundable deposit.

Please contact Samuel French for perusal of the music materials as well as a performance license application.

IMPORTANT BILLING AND CREDIT REQUIREMENTS

All producers of *MUSICAL OF MUSICALS THE MUSICAL must* give credit to the Author of the Play in all programs distributed in connection with performances of the Play, and in all instances in which the title of the Play appears for the purposes of advertising, publicizing or otherwise exploiting the Play and/or a production. The name of the Author *must* appear on a separate line on which no other name appears, immediately following the title and *must* appear in size of type not less than fifty percent of the size of the title type.

Billing *must* be substantially as follows:

(Name of Producer)

Presents

MUSICAL OF MUSICALS
THE MUSICAL!

Music by   Lyrics by
Eric Rockwell   **Joanne Bogart**

Book by
Eric Rockwell and Joanne Bogart

In addition the following credit *must* be given in all programs and publicity information distributed in association with this piece:

Original New York Production by THE YORK THEATRE COMPANY
James Morgan, Producing Artistic Director
Comercially Produced in NYC by Melanie Herman

ARTWORK REQUIREMENT

The New York Producers have generously made available the original title graphic and artwork from the New York production of the Play. All licensees of MUSICAL OF MUSICALS are requested to use this approved title graphic and artwork in all advertising, press and marketing of the Play.

Please contact Samuel French, Inc. for more information and to obtain copies of approved artwork.

Opening night, February 10th, 2005

DODGER STAGES
340 West 50th Street

THE YORK THEATRE COMPANY and MELANIE HERMAN
PRESENT

THE MUSICAL OF MUSICALS
THE MUSICAL!

PRODUCED BY
MELANIE HERMAN
W. DAVID McCOY and JAMES MORGAN
ASSOCIATE PRODUCER LENNY DEMEYER

MUSIC BY
ERIC ROCKWELL

LYRICS BY
JOANNE BOGART

BOOK BY
ROCKWELL & BOGART

WITH
JOANNE BOGART CRAIG FOLS LOVETTE GEORGE ERIC ROCKWELL

SCENIC DESIGN	LIGHTING DESIGN	COSTUME DESIGN	SOUND DESIGN
JAMES MORGAN	**MARY JO DONDLINGER**	**JOHN CARVER SULLIVAN**	**DAVID GOTWALD**

PRESS REPRESENTATIVE	GENERAL MANAGER	ADDITIONAL CASTING	MARKETING	PRODUCTION STAGE MANAGER
HELENE DAVIS	**MARTIAN ENTERTAINMENT, INC**	**NORMAN MERANUS**	**MARTIAN MEDIA**	**B.J. FORMAN**
	CARL D. WHITE TOM SMEDES		ERIN AUERBACH MAX WIXOM	

DIRECTED AND CHOREOGRAPHED BY
PAMELA HUNT

Original Cast Album on JAY CDs

Original New York production by THE YORK THEATRE COMPANY, James Morgan, Producing Artistic Director

CAST

ACT I

CORN — *In the Style of Rodgers & Hammerstein*

Big Willy	CRAIG FOLS
June	LOVETTE GEORGE
Jidder	ERIC ROCKWELL
Mother Abby	JOANNE BOGART

A LITTLE COMPLEX — *In the Style of Stephen Sondheim*

Jitter	ERIC ROCKWELL
Jeune	LOVETTE GEORGE
Billy	CRAIG FOLS
Abby	JOANNE BOGART

DEAR ABBY— *In the Style of Jerry Herman*

Auntie Abby	JOANNE BOGART
Junie Faye	LOVETTE GEORGE
William	CRAIG FOLS
Mr. Jitters	ERIC ROCKWELL

ACT II

ASPECTS OF JUNITA—*In the Style of Andrew Lloyd Webber*

Junita	LOVETTE GEORGE
Bill	CRAIG FOLS
Phantom Jitter	ERIC ROCKWELL
Abigail Von Schtarr	JOANNE BOGART

SPEAKEASY— *In the Style of Kander & Ebb*

Jütter	ERIC ROCKWELL
Juny	LOVETTE GEORGE
Villy	CRAIG FOLS
Fraulein Abby	JOANNE BOGART

CHORUS

(Really good actors like the ones listed never appear in the chorus unless it turns out that, well, they have to. And then they do so only grudgingly.)

Farmer 1, Cowman 1, Neurotic New Yorker 1, Party Guest 2, Chorus Boy 1, Roller Skater 3, Argentinean 1; Snowball the Cat, Slutty Dancing Girl 1...CRAIG FOLS

Farmwoman 1, Towns woman 1, Neurotic New Yorker 2, Party Guest 1, Killer Soprano, Argentinean 2, Roller Skater 2, Frisky the Cat, Slutty Dancing Girl 2...............................LOVETTE GEORGE

Farmer who plays piano, Cowman who plays piano, Neurotic New York Pianist, Roller Skating Pianist, Argentinean Pianist, Kitten on the Keys, Man at Piano, Piano Man..................ERIC ROCKWELL

Older Farmwoman, Older Townswoman, Older Neurotic New Yorker, Older Roller Skater, Older Argentinean, Methuselah the Cat, Older Slutty Dancing Girl, Older Than Springtime, Old Man River, Old Battle-axe, Old Crone, Old Bag, Old Frump, Old Broad...JOANNE BOGART

A NOTE FROM THE AUTHORS

The Musical of Musicals (The Musical) can be produced and directed in a variety of ways. The Off-Broadway production featured a cast of four, which included the two of us playing the roles of Jitter and Abby. The piano was onstage, with each actor taking turns providing the accompaniment. The four actors also doubled as the chorus. This concept worked well.

But *The Musical of Musicals (The Musical)* need not be limited to a small cast of piano-playing performers. In fact, the show could work well with a large ensemble supporting four leading players in the roles of Willy, June, Abby and Jitter. While the Off-Broadway version kept production values to a minimum, your production could incorporate different sets and costumes for each style.

Throughout the script you will see many stage directions, which were spoken aloud by the pianist in the off-Broadway version. These could be spoken by a separate actor, the pianist, or divided up among the cast. Or they could be heard from a disembodied voice coming from the heavens. In addition, each variation is preceded by the words "in the style of ...". This is important information for the audience to know. In the Off-Broadway production, these words were seen before each segment via projections. However, you may choose another way of presenting them visually, or you may choose to have them spoken.

One word of warning concerns performance and direction. In shows like this one, there is often a temptation to play it as a show gone awry, with staged accidents and collisions, purposefully bad acting and singing, and choreographed mistakes. Don't give into this temptation! These five variations are satires of great musical theatre, and it works best if they are performed and directed as if they are five great works of art. This is not a parody of amateur theatre, but of Broadway theatre. So give it your best.

Here are some additional notes for actors to keep in mind. Since each character is actually an amalgam of various characters from various shows, it is not a good idea to do impressions of any one particular performer. It's fine to toss off an occasional line or lyric or physical gesture that calls to mind a specific actor, but be judicious.

Another point is to make your characters very distinct in each of the five sections. A different acting style is called for in each variation. If you're playing June, for example, your R&H ingénue is completely sweet and sincere (although your lyrics are silly) while your Junita in the ALW is strident and commanding (although your lyrics are silly). In other words, play them for real in the style appropriate to the writer, but don't comment on it. The lines and lyrics are doing all the commenting.

As for direction and choreography, the same stylistic approach applies. Just as each actor is given the opportunity to work in five different styles, so, too, are the director, choreographer and designers. For example, dance styles run the gamut from Agnes DeMille to Bob Fosse.

In the words of Stephen Sondheim, "Every minor detail is a major decision," and every minor detail in this show is part of a distinctive style. If the production team does their job well, your audience will be getting five musicals for the price of one!

SPECIAL MARKETING NOTE

In addition to the ARTWORK REQUIREMENT listed on page 3, The producers of the New York production request and recommend that you please consider the critically acclaimed New York Production Director and Design Team to be utilized in the mounting of your production of THE MUSICAL OF MUSICALS (THE MUSICAL!), if reasonably possible for you to do so. Although not an obligation for a license, the Producers make this recommendation to assist and support your licensed production, and further, to help you in your efforts to achieve critical and financial success.

For more information on the New York Production Director and Designers, marketing, advertising, sales and branding tactics, and for questions and further information, please feel free to contact Melanie Herman, Producer, at 212.224.0319 x 14 (MHerman@CorporateLeisureTravel.com) or Carl D. White, General Manager, Martian Entertainment LLC at 212.302.4848 (cwhite@martianentertainment.com).
Or log onto our website at www.TheMusicalofMusicals.com.

ACT I

Five Musicals! One Plot!

CAST.
THE MUSICAL OF MUSICALS!
MUSICAL, MUSICAL, MUSICAL!

WE'RE SINGING!
THAT'S BECAUSE IT'S A MUSICAL!
AND IN A MUSICAL
EVERYONE SINGS!

OH, MUSICAL!
WE LOVE YOU SO!
SO LET'S GET ON WITH THE SHOW!

THE MUSICAL OF MUSICALS!

(Blackout)

Scene: *Corn!*
In the Style of Rodgers and Hammerstein

(As the lights come up, ABBY is revealed churning butter.)

SPOKEN STAGE DIRECTION. The lights come up on a farm. Beyond it, fields of golden corn stretch out to the horizon. It is Kansas in August.

(BIG WILLY begins to sing offstage.)

BIG WILLY.
THE EARTH SPINS AROUND LIKE A CAROUSEL

9

ON BRIGHT CLOUDS OF MUSIC WE FLY
(BIG WILLY enters.)
THE CATTLE PLIÉ IN A DREAMY BALLET
IT'S NORMAL AS BLUEBERRY PIE

OH, WHAT BEAUTIFUL CORN
WHAT BEAUTIFUL, BEAUTIFUL CORN
THE WIND WHISPERS SECRETS, THE FIELD IS ALL EARS
OH, WHAT BEAUTIFUL CORN

    BIG WILLY. Mornin', Miss Abby.
    ABBY. Mornin', Big Willy.

    BIG WILLY.
FARMIN' THE LAND IS THE LIFE FOR ME
IT CALLS ME AND I CAIN'T SAY NO
BUT I'D GLADLY FORSAKE ANY SHOVEL OR RAKE
I'M IN LOVE WITH A WONDERFUL HOE

OH, WHAT BEAUTIFUL CORN
WHAT BEAUTIFUL, BEAUTIFUL CORN
I SAID IT BEFORE AND I'LL SAY IT AGAIN
OH, WHAT BEAUTIFUL CORN!

ALL THE CRITTERS ARE HAVIN' A FIELD DAY
THE DONKEYS HEE-HAWIN' WITH GLEE
A GAGGLE O'GEESE ARE A-GIGGLIN'
HESH UP YOU HYENA! STOP LAUGHIN' AT ME!

OH THE CHIPMUNK IS READIN' THE BIBLE
WELL, NOW THERE'S A REMARKABLE THOUGHT
GUESS HE LEARNED IT THE SAME WAY A LARK LEARNS
    TO PRAY
HE'S GOT TO BE CAREFULLY TAUGHT

OH, WHAT BEAUTIFUL CORN
WHAT BEAUTIFUL, BEAUTIFUL CORN
WHAT'S THIS IN MY TOOTH? IT'S A KERNEL OF TRUTH
SHUCKS, WHAT BEAUTIFUL CORN

WHAT BEAUTIFUL, BEAUTIFUL, BEAUTIFUL, BEAUTIFUL
BEAUTIFUL, BEAUTIFUL, BEAUTIFUL, BEAUTIFUL
BEAUTIFUL, BEAUTIFUL, BEAUTIFUL, BEAUTIFUL
BEAUTIFUL, BEAUTIFUL CORN!

ABBY. Mornin', Big Willy. Come to call on June?

BIG WILLY. Heck no, Miss Abby. What use have I got for her? I got my life all figgered out. Travelin' with the carnival, seein' the world, *(Takes 'King and I' pose with hands on hips.)* et cetera, et cetera, et cetera.

ABBY. Sounds like you're high as an elephant's eye! You young-uns don't fool me none. Never seen two dang fools more in love. *(JUNE enters.)* June, look who's here!

BIG WILLY. Mornin', June.

(ABBY exits.)

JUNE. What're you doin' here?

BIG WILLY. I was just wanderin' around yer cornfield!

JUNE. Oh, what's the use of wanderin?

YOU SPEND SO MUCH TIME IN THE CORNFIELD
FOLKS'RE STARTIN' TO TALK.
THERE'S NOTHIN' BUT HUSKS AND KERNALS AND COBS
AND ALL THE REST IS STALK!

BIG WILLY. I couldn't keer less what folks'll say...

JUNE. And I couldn't keer less about you!

I COULDN'T KEER LESS ABOUT YOU.
I COULDN'T KEER LESS ABOUT YOU.
AND TO SHOW YOU HOW LITTLE I DO
I'LL WASH MY SOCKS AND COMB MY HAIR,
AND RINSE OUT MY LONG UNDERWEAR,
I'LL SHAVE MY LEGS AND PIERCE MY EARS,
AND BUY SOME FANCY NEW BRASSIERES,
I'LL PLUCK MY BROWS AND MY NOSE HAIRS, TOO
'CAUSE I COULDN'T KEER LESS ABOUT YOU!

BIG WILLY. Say, you tryin' to git me to marry you? Well, I won't, see?
I DON'T LOVE YOU
THOUGH PEOPLE WILL SAY THAT I DO.
OH, I DON'T LOVE YOU
AND I HOPE THAT YOU DON'T LOVE ME TOO.
IF I DID, WHICH I DON'T,
I WOULD TELL YOU SO.
BUT I DON'T, SO I WON'T.
OKAY, NOW YOU KNOW.
I DON'T LOVE YOU.

    SPOKEN STAGE DIRECTION. The landlord enters.
    JUNE. You gave me such a fright! Big Willy, this is…
    JIDDER. They call me Jidder.
    JUNE. You come to collect the rent, I s'pose?
    JIDDER. That's right, Miss High and Mighty! And if I don't collect it by 5 o'clock today, I'm gonna marry you myself, you understand?
    BIG WILLY. Hey, leave the little lady alone!
    JIDDER. What's it to you, Mr. High and Mighty?
    BIG WILLY. Well, you cain't up and marry her jest 'cause she cain't pay her rent!
    JIDDER. Oh, cain't I? It says I can right here in this Lease!
    BIG WILLY. That lease'll never hold up in court!
    JIDDER. Yes it will. And don't call me Liesl! So either I see the rent, or I'll see ya at the weddin'! And now I'm goin' back to my dark and lonely room. To look at pictures. Pictures of *dirty girls*.

(He exits.)

    JUNE. That Jidder is up to no good. But I guess I have to marry him, since you don't love me and I don't love you!
    BIG WILLY. Okay, Okay, Okay!
    JUNE. Don't throw Okays at me!
    BIG WILLY. Well, if that's the way you want it, so long!
    JUNE. Farewell!
    BIG WILLY. Auf Wiedersehen!

JUNE. Good bye!
BOTH.
I DON'T LOVE YOU!

(BIG WILLY exits. ABBY enters.)

JUNE. Oh, Abby...*Mother* Abby, I'm so confused. Should I follow my heart and marry Big Willy or follow my head and marry Jidder?

MOTHER ABBY.
THERE'S A RAINBOW O'ER THE MOUNTAIN
AND THAT RAINBOW IS YOUR DREAM.
YOU'LL FIND IT WHEN YOU'VE FACED THE STORM
AND FORDED EVERY STREAM.
SILVER LARKS WILL SERENADE YOU
ON THAT ISLAND OF YOUR DREAM,
THAT ISLAND WITH THE MOUNTAIN AND
THE RAINBOW AND THE STREAM.

FOLLOW YOUR DREAM
DON'T ASK ME WHY
FOLLOW YOUR DREAM
UNTIL YOU DIE

WALK ON THROUGH THE WIND AND TRUDGE THROUGH
    THE RAIN
THOUGH YOUR HAIR'S ALL BLOWN AND YOU LOOK
    INSANE
AND YOUR EYE MAKE-UP'S RUNNING AND YOUR NOSE
    IS RED.
THE HILLS ARE ALIVE BUT YOU'RE HALF DEAD!

FOLLOW YOUR DREAM
CHIN UP! BELLY HIGH!
FOLLOW YOUR DREAM
UNTIL YOU DIE,
YOU DIE, YOU DIE, YOU DIE. YOU DIE,
DREAM UNTIL YOU DIE!!!!

JUNE. Thank you, Mother Abby. That was so helpful. *(ABBY exits.)* Hmmm. Follow my dream...dream...dream...

SPOKEN STAGE DIRECTION. As June drifts off to sleep, in her own little corner, in her own little chair, Dream June appears. *(Ballet begins.)* Dream Willy enters. Together, they dance a highly symbolic ballet. Sort of 'Run of DeMille'. Dream Mother Abby crosses, bringing corn to all. June marches down the aisle holding a bouquet of corn. Dream Jidder marries Dream June. Dream Jidder tears up the lease. *(The ballet ends.)* June awakens to find Jidder standing in front of her.

JIDDER. Time's up, Miss High and Mighty. You got the rent?

JUNE. But Jidder, you tore up the lease, remember?

JIDDER. That wasn't me. That was *Dream* Jidder. If you ain't got the rent then you're comin' with me. To git married!

JUNE. But, why me, Jidder?

JIDDER. Because you're June! June, June, June! Jest because yer June!

(He carries her over his shoulder.)

JUNE. Put me down!

JIDDER. Okay. You're nothin' but a no-good low-down flib-berty-jibbert!

JUNE. No, put me *down*.

JIDDER. Oh. All right, Miss High and Mighty. Now where in tarnation is that Parson?

(BIG WILLY enters as JUNE and JIDDER exit.)

BIG WILLY. *(Calls after them.)* Hey! That's my girl! I'll just go and get her! Or...Is a puzzlement!

IF I GIT HER I'LL HAVE TO STAY.
IF NOT, I'LL BE ON MY WAY.

SHOULD I STAY OR SHOULD I GO?
IS IT YES OR IS IT NO?

TO BE OR NOT TO BE?
IT'S TIME FOR MY SOLILOQUY!

She can't tie me down! I gotta see the world!

IF I GO, I'LL BE FREE TO RAMBLE,
TO DRINK AND CUSS AND GAMBLE,
SHOWIN' HOW MANLY I AM.
GOT MORE GIRLS THAN THE KING OF SIAM!

Still…
IF I STAY, I CAN HAVE LOTS OF CORN —
CORN FROM NIGHT TILL MORN!

Say, maybe that's too much corn! Besides, it's hard work to live on
a farm.

THERE'S CHORES – LIKE MILKIN' OL BESSIE,
A-KICKIN' AND A-SQUIRTIN' 'ROUND THE PLACE.
I'D SURE BE LOOKIN' ALL MESSY
WITH A POUND AND A HALF OF CREAM UPON MY FACE.

Well, maybe it's time I settle down. June sure is purty. We could
have a son. I'll name him after me!

I'LL TEACH HIM TO WRASSLE AND PLAY.
SOME FELLERS MIGHT THINK IT'S SILLY
FOR A BIG GUY LIKE ME TO STAY HOME ALL DAY
PLAYIN' WITH MY OWN LITTLE WILLY.

Well, so what?

I GOTTA DECIDE.
I CAN'T STAY TORN.
I'LL POP THE QUESTION,
IF SHE'LL POP THE CORN!
I SWEAR BY AN ELEPHANT'S EYE

I'LL SAY "I DO" OR DIE!
Or should I?

(He exits.)

SPOKEN STAGE DIRECTION. Lights up back on the farm, following the wedding of Jidder and June. *(Chorus enters.)* The townsfolk are celebrating.

CHORUS.
THAT WAS DELICIOUS CLAM DIP
EATING IT MADE US GLAD
WE KNOW THEY WERE MINCED, BUT WE'RE CONVINCED
THAT SOME OF THEM CLAMS WERE BAD
OUR STOMACHS HURT, OUR BLADDERS ARE FULL
WE DRANK TOO MUCH CHAMPAGNE
THAT WAS DELICIOUS CLAM DIP
BUT SOME OF US GOT PTOMAINE

SOLO.
REMEMBER WHEN WE OPENED UP THE CORN CHIP BAG
    AND POURED 'EM ALL INTO A BOWL
THEN WE GOBBLED AND GULPED AND CRUNCHED AND
    MUNCHED
GUESS WE JUST LOST CONTROL

CHORUS.
GOBBLIN' AND A-GULPIN'
CRUNCHIN' AND A-MUNCHIN'
LOSIN' OUR SELF-CONTROL

SOLO.
I'D LIKE TO SAY A WORD FOR GUACAMOLE...

(BIG WILLY enters.)

BIG WILLY. Wait! Stop the weddin'!
JUNE. Oh, Big Willy! I knew you'd come. But it's too late —
Jidder and me are already married.

JIDDER. That's right, Mr. High and Mighty. She's mine. It says so right here on this marriage certificate. We're legally wed as of 5 o'clock today!

JUNE. I- gu-guess this is go-good-bye Big Willy.

BIG WILLY. I gu-guess so...

BOTH.
I DON'T LOVE...

ABBY. Wait! Let me see that certificate. Hah! Why this scrap o' paper don't mean nuthin'. Haven't y'all heard? Kansas has adopted Daylight Savings Time!

CHORUS. Daylight Savings Time?!?

JUNE. Well that means it's only10 after 4. So we ain't married yet!

JIDDER. But ya still gotta pay the rent!

BIG WILLY. I'll pay the rent! And well before 5'oclock!

ALL.
DAYLIGHT SAVINGS TIME SAVED THE DAY!
DAYLIGHT SAVINGS TIME SAVED THE DAY!

CHORUS MAN.
THERE'S AN EXTRA HOUR
SO HE CAN MARRY MAY.

JUNE.
JUNE!

CHORUS WOMAN.
WE CAN TURN OUR CLOCKS BACK
THEN THROW 'EM ALL AWAY.

CHORUS MAN.
THEY'LL BE MAKIN' WHOOPEE,

ALL.
WE'LL ALL BE MAKIN' HAY!

DAYLIGHT SAVINGS, DAYLIGHT SAVINGS,
DAYLIGHT SAVINGS, DAYLIGHT SAVINGS TIME
DAYLIGHT SAVINGS TIME SAVED THE
D-A-Y-L-I-G-H-T-S-A-V-I-N-G-S-T-I-M-E DAY!!!!

JIDDER. Now wait just a minute, Mother High and Mighty....Aaaaaagh!

SPOKEN STAGE DIRECTION. Jidder trips and falls on his own knife.

JUNE. Oh. Jidder tripped and fell on his own knife. He's dead. (*Quickly recovering*). So Big Willy, what were you asking me before?

BIG WILLY. Whaddya say? Will you marry me, June? June, June, June?

JUNE. Yes. Yes, yes, yes!

ALL.
OH WHAT BEAUTIFUL CORN
WHAT BEAUTIFUL, BEAUTIFUL, BEAUTIFUL, BEAUTIFUL...

(*Chorus drops out.*)

JUNE.
(*Hysterically*)
BEAUTIFUL, BEAUTIFUL, BEAUTIFUL, BEAUTIFUL
(*Piano drops out.*)
BEAUTIFUL, BEAUT...

(*WILLY slaps her.*)

Sometimes you can get hit. Hit real hard. And it feels like a kiss...

ALL.
WHAT BEAUTIFUL CORN!

(*Blackout*)

Scene: *A Little Complex*
In the Style of Stephen Sondheim

SPOKEN STAGE DIRECTION. The lights come up on a New York City apartment complex, aptly called "The Woods". The company of actors sets the scene.

JITTER.
IRONY
AMBIGUITY
DISSONANCE
ANGST

CHORUS.
WELCOME TO OUR COMPLEX
OUR APARTMENT COMPLEX
WELCOME TO "THE WOODS"

(The following can be divided into solos, duets, or other vocal combinations)

ALL OF OUR TENANTS ARE VERY NEUROTIC
EMOTIONAL LIVES ARE COMPLETELY CHAOTIC
THE SONGS IN THEIR HEARTS AREN'T EVER MELODIC
EVERYONE HERE IS A LITTLE BIT LOST
IN THE WOODS
WELCOME TO "THE WOODS"

THE SENTIMENTS HEARD HERE ARE SELDOM ENDEARING
IT'S KIND OF SLOW GOING, BUT WORTH PERSEVERING
IT MAY NOT SINK IN TILL THE THIRD OR FOURTH HEARING
THEN IF YOU'RE BRIGHT, THERE'S A GLIMMER OF LIGHT
IN THE WOODS
WELCOME TO "THE WOODS"

DON'T FEEL OBTUSE
YES, IT'S ABSTRUSE
EVERY ONE HERE HAS AT LEAST ONE SCREW LOOSE

UNLIKEABLE PEOPLE WITH LIVES THAT ARE HOLLOW
IT'S ALL FOOD FOR THOUGHT, BUT A BIT HARD TO SWAL-
    LOW
SO DON'T FEEL TOO BAD IF YOU DON'T REALLY FOLLOW
YOU'RE NOT ALONE, BUT THEN NO ONE'S ALONE
IN THE WOODS
WELCOME TO "THE WOODS"

APARTMENT 60 - ABBY

SHE'S BITTER AND BOOZY
A BIT OF A FLOOZY
SHE'S BLOWZY AND FROWZY
AND NOT VERY CHOOSY

APARTMENT 75 - BILLY

HE WANTS TO WRITE SONGS BUT
THE PROSPECTS ARE DISMAL
HIS THOUGHTS ARE SO DEEP THAT
IN FACT THEY'RE ABYSMAL

APARTMENT 73 - JEUNE

FINANCES RESTRICTED,
EMOTIONS CONFLICTED,
SHE WANDERS AND WONDERS
WHEN SHE'LL BE EVICTED

BY THE LANDLORD
THERE'S ALWAYS A LANDLORD
BUT WHO IS THE LANDLORD?
JITTER, JITTER, *JITTER!!!*

LET US CONSIDER THE STORY OF JITTER
SOME HAD MISTAKEN HIS ART FOR LITTER
HE LEFT IT OUT IN THE HALL ONE DAY
AND WHEN HE RETURNED THEY HAD THROWN IT AWAY

THEY THOUGHT HIS ART WAS PIECE OF JUNK
THEY THREW IT OUT IN A HUNK, KERPLUNK
AND WHEN HE FOUND OUT HE GOT DRUNK AS A SKUNK
JITTER — THE LANDLORD SLASH ARTIST SLASH DEMON.

SOLO.
HE SITS IN HIS APARTMENT
WOND'RING WHERE HIS ART WENT

(Chorus exits.)

JITTER.
I'M MADDER THAN A HATTER — I'M ABOUT TO SPLIT
    HEADS
LIVING IN A BUILDING THAT IS FILLED WITH SHITHEADS

Fools. They've destroyed my masterpiece. They must die.

I SWEAR BY THE GODS OF MURDER AND ART
I'LL TAKE MY REVENGE ON THOSE WHO TOOK PART
I'LL MAKE THEM PAY
IN A CRAFTY WAY
I'LL KILL THEM AND COAT THEM WITH PAPIER MÂCHÉ
I KNOW THEY SAY
I'M NO MONET
QUE SERA, QUE SEURAT, OH, WHAT THE HAY

*(JEUNE rings JITTER'S custom-made doorbell: Sound effect of
  · shrieking factory whistle as used in Sweeney Todd.)*

JITTER. The doorbell. Go away!!!

(JEUNE enters.)

JEUNE. Hi, I'm Jeune. I hate to disturb you while you're busy
brooding, but I need to speak to you. Oh, what a lovely color
scheme. Red, red, red, red, red, blue, blue, blue, blue, picks up the
orange, picks up the orange...
    JITTER. What do you want?
    JEUNE. I know I'm behind in my rent, but I'll pay as soon as

I can.

JITTER. *(Menacingly)* Perhaps there's another solution. In lieu of paying your rent, why don't you pose for me?

JEUNE. Why, Jitter. Show a little decorum.

JITTER. A funny thing happened on the way to decorum. Will you pose for me?

JEUNE. Oh, I don't know... I want to. No, I don't. I thought I did, but now I'm not so sure...
SOMETIMES I THINK I'M HAVING A THOUGHT
BUT THEN, I REALIZE I'M NOT
YOU SEE, I HAVE BIRDS

JITTER. Birds?

JEUNE.
I HAVE LITTLE BIRDS
FLYING 'ROUND MY HEAD
WHY DO THE BIRDS, FLY
AROUND MY GOLDEN HAIR?
ARE THEY BUILDING NESTS UP THERE?
WITH TWIGS AND SPRIGS AND BITS OF TWINE
WHO CLEANS THE MESSES
THEY LEAVE IN MY TRESSES
YOUR GUESS IS AS GOOD AS MINE
FLY, LITTLE BIRDS, FLY
DON'T POKE ME IN THE EYE
IT'S HARD TO HEAR YOUR WORDS
AS I MIGHT HAVE SAID
WITH ALL THESE LITTLE BIRDS
FLYING 'ROUND MY HEAD

JITTER. I want you to pose for me — so I can sneak up behind you, slit your throat and cover your corpse with papier mâché.

CHORUS.
JITTER IS CRAZY. HE'S *CRAZY!!!*

JITTER.
WHAT WOULD BE THE MATTER
WITH THE MURDER OF A MODEL?
IF THE MODEL WERE A MORON
IN THE MIDDLE OF A MUDDLE?

THE ART OF RETRIBUTION
DEPENDS ON EXECUTION.

Ah, getting away with murder! *(Savagely to a man in the front row.)*
But, tell me, Mister, how shall I do her in? Bake her into a pie, perhaps? No! I need...I need...an epiphany!

SHALL I USE A KNIFE?
NOT ON YOUR LIFE!
TO SLASH IN A PASSION
IS SO OUT OF FASHION.

SHALL I USE A GUN?
FUN, BUT OVERDONE.
TO SHOOT DOESN'T SUIT HER
THIS SUITOR'S ASTUTER

WOULD IT BE TOO GRIM
TO TEAR HER LIMB FROM LIMB?
ALARMING, YET CHARMING
AND TRULY DIS-ARMING!

SHALL I USE A ROPE?
SHOOT HER UP WITH DOPE?
HEMLOCK IS EASY
BUT TOO SOCRATES-Y
HATS OFF TO DECAPITATION!

SHE'LL BE DEAD
AND I'LL GET A HEAD
I'LL TRY NOT TO GLOAT
AS MY KNIFE

Hey old friend, what do you say old friend?

SLITS HER THROA…

(Sound effect - Factory Whistle doorbell cuts off his last note.)

JEUNE. Oh. *(Cheerily)* Phones ring, doors chime, in comes
company. Come on in.

(BILLY enters.)

BILLY. Hi!
JEUNE. Bill. Billy.

BILLY-BABY, BILLY-BUBI
WILLY. SILLY-WILLY, WILLY-NILLY, WOOLY-BULLY
WILLY. WILLIE WINKIE. WILLIE WONKA…

JITTER. All right! Well, what do you want, "Billy-Baby"?
BILLY. I came to check up on Jeune. It sounded like you were
making some pretty specific overtures. Jeune, I've written another
song and I'm dedicating it to you, babe.

YOU'RE LIKE A MELODY
A MEMORABLE MELODY
A TUNEFUL MELODY
A HUMMABLE MELODY…

JITTER. Stop! You'll never win her back with that sentimen-
tal tripe. She's mine.
JEUNE. But Jitter, Billy might find me a place where I can pay
the rent.
JITTER. Careful.

FINDERS CAN BE WEEPERS
LOSERS CAN BE KEEPERS
ROSES CAN BE RED
VIOLETS CAN BE BLUE
SOME LYRICS RHYME
SOME DON'T

ARE YOU WITH ME?
STAY WITH ME

    JEUNE. And what does all that mean?

I'M WEARY BEING WARY

    JITTER.
BE WARY OF THE WEARY

    BILLY.
DON'T WORRY IF IT'S SCARY

    JITTER.
BUT SCARY ISN'T EERIE
BE LEERY OF THE WARY
ARE YOU WITH ME?
STAY WITH ME.

    JEUNE.
THIS IS ALL TOO DEEP
I'M FALLING ASLEEP

    BILLY. No!

WHEN YOU HAVE TO STRAIN
TO EXPLAIN
THE ARCANE
IT'S BOUND
TO SOUND
PROFOUND
ARE YOU WITH ME?
STAY WITH ME.

Jeune, wake up. Let's get out of here. He's crazy.

    JITTER. Crazy?

I AM NOT A LOON
TRULY

NO ONE IS A LOON
STAY WITH ME

Well, Jeune, who are you going to stay with?

> **JEUNE.** Oh, I don't know…well, Billy and I are engaged.
> **JITTER.** You're marrying that hack? Out, I say, OUT!!!

> **CHORUS.**
JITTER'S STILL CRAZY. HE'S *CRAZY*!!!

> **BILLY.** Listen, babe. You'd better decide. It's either Jitter or
me!

(He exits.)

> **SPOKEN STAGE DIRECTION.** Later that day, Jeune
knocks on her neighbor's door.
> **ABBY.** Yeah, what?
> **JEUNE.** Abby, I need your advice.

TELL ME WHAT TO DO
BECAUSE I DON'T KNOW WHAT TO DO
I REALLY THINK I'M GOING CRAZY
LIKE THAT WOMAN IN THE SHOE
I MEAN I DON'T HAVE ALL THOSE CHILDREN YET
I'M ONLY THIRTY-TWO
YET I'M ENGAGED TO MARRY BILL
BUT NOW I'M FOND OF JITTER TOO
ALTHOUGH I THINK HE WANTS TO KILL ME
'CAUSE I HAVEN'T PAID MY RENT YET
AND I THREW HIS PRICELESS ARTWORK
IN THE DUMPER WITH THE OTHER GARBAGE

I HAVE BIRDS, AND I'M NOT VERY LUCID
I HAVE BIR…

> **ABBY.** Wait! I'd like to propose a test: Let's see what would
happen if you shut up!

SO YOU'RE CONFUSED
BIG DEAL
SO WHAT
WHO'S NOT?
GO TAKE A CLASS IN POTTERY
WIN THE LOTTERY
HAVE ANOTHER DRINK, WE'LL TOAST TO CAMARADERIE
YOU'RE BRINGIN' A TEAR TO MY EYE
DON'T YOU GET IT SWEETY-PIE?
WE'RE ALL GONNA DIE!

YOU DON'T BELIEVE ME?
JUST WATCH THE CLOCK
TICK TOCK
IT'S ALL A CROCK

YOU'RE PERPLEXED
NEWS FLASH—
WHO CARES?
SAVE YOUR PRAYERS
NEXT TIME YOU PASS A CASKET BY
STOP AND ASK, "DO I
REALLY HAVE TO DIE?"
WELL, YOU CAN KISS YOUR ASS GOOD-BYE
WHY EVEN BOTHER TO TRY?
LIFE SUCKS AND YOU WANNA KNOW WHY?
WE'RE ALL GONNA DIE! DIE!! DIE!!!

JEUNE. Thank you Abby. That was so helpful.

BILLY. Hi girls. I just sold that hummable melody song. I'll pay the rent.

JEUNE. Oh Billy. Let's all go tell Jitter we're sorry. Uh, grateful.

(They exit.)

SPOKEN STAGE DIRECTION. Warily, they stroll along to Jitter's apartment.

JITTER. My hour of revenge has come. They must all die so my art can live. But how much longer can I wait?

(JEUNE. BILLY and ABBY enter, preparing to ring his doorbell.)

THE END IS NEAR
I WILL PERSEVERE
GOD, MAKE ME PATIENT—

(Sound effect — Factory Whistle doorbell.)

DON'T BOTHER — THEY'RE HERE.

    CHORUS.
THAT'S WHEN HE MURDERED THE THREE HELPLESS
    TENANTS
JITTER'S IN JAIL NOW — HE'S DOING HIS PENANCE
HE TURNED THEM ALL INTO OBJETS D'ART
ALL RIGHT, SO THE PLOT GOT A LITTLE BIZARRE
THIS GORY STORY OF ART AND CRIME
IS MORE RIDICULOUS THAN SUBLIME
BUT LUCKILY THIS IS THE VERY LAST RHYME.
(TILL NEXT TIME.)

(Blackout)

Scene: *Dear Abby!*
In the Style of Jerry Herman

    SPOKEN STAGE DIRECTION. The lights come up on a party at Abby's swank penthouse apartment. Everyone is drinking martinis.

    CHORUS.
WHERE'S THE LIFE OF THE PARTY?
WHERE'S THE TOAST OF THE TOWN?
SOON SHE'LL MAKE HER BIG ENTRANCE IN A FABULOUS
    GOWN
WE DON'T KNOW HOW TO HANDLE
OUR DRAB AND DREARY LIVES
UNTIL THE LIFE OF THE PARTY ARRIVES.

SPOKEN STAGE DIRECTION. Abby appears at the top of a staircase. The audience applauds wildly, even though she hasn't done anything yet.

CHORUS. Abby!

ABBY.
LIFE'S FULL OF GLAMOUR AND SPARKLE AND ZEST
TAKE MY ADVICE AND LIVE!

CHORUS. Hey Abby!

ABBY.
START BLOWIN' YOUR BUGLE AND DON'T BE DEPRESSED

CHORUS. Abby!

ABBY.
TAKE MY ADVICE AND LIVE!

CHORUS. Hey look there's Abby!

ABBY.
WATCH ME STRUT 'CAUSE I'M AN OLD PRO
I CAN'T SING OR DANCE, BUT I'M THE STAR OF THE
    SHOW

CHORUS.
SO WHILE SHE'S GOT IT TO GIVE
TAKE HER ADVICE AND LIVE!

START CRASHIN' THE CYMBALS AND BEATIN' THE BAND
TAKE HER ADVICE AND LIVE *(Let's start livin')*
WE'RE KICKIN' OUR HEELS UP SO GIVE US A HAND
TAKE HER ADVICE AND LIVE! *(Live! Live! Live!)*

ABBY.
AND IF I SHOULD WANDER TOO FAR ASTRAY
MY CHORUS BOYS'LL COME AND I'LL GET CARRIED

AWAY

CHORUS.
SO WHILE SHE'S GOT IT TO GIVE
TAKE HER ADVICE AND LIVE, LIVE, LIVE, LIVE, LIVE,
LIVE, LIVE, LIVE, LIVE, LIVE, LIVE, LIVE...

ABBY. Life is a star vehicle — and most poor suckers are in a bus and truck!

CHORUS.
LIVE!

JUNIE. *(Nasally)* Oh, Abby.
ABBY. Yes, Junie Faye?
JUNIE. I have a cold in my nose, a crick in my neck, and ribbons down my back. And I can't pay my rent! What do I do now?
ABBY. I want you to meet my nephew, William. My, what a lovely couple you make. *(To audience.)* See? It only takes a moment. Now, I'm going to rejoin the human race, if you'll have me!
SPOKEN STAGE DIRECTION. *(As ABBY exits.)* She acknowledges her exit applause.
JUNIE. My, what lovely knickers you're wearing.
WILLIAM. Aunt Abby says I can have long pants on my fortieth birthday! Oh, Boy! June, you make me wanna...
JUNIE. Wanna...?

WILLIAM.
YOU MAKE ME WANNA SING A SHOW TUNE
THE KIND THAT USED TO BE ALL THE RAGE
A GOOD OLD HUMMABLE, LIFTABLE SHOWTUNE
THERE'S NO REASON FOR THE RHYMIN'
'CAUSE WE'RE ONLY MARKIN' TIME UN-
TIL THE STAR GETS BACK ON STAGE

JUNIE. Does this mean you can pay my rent for me?
WILLIAM. Gosh, I'd love to, but my allowance is only 10 cents a week.
JUNIE. Don't you have a job?

WILLIAM. No. All I do is mix martinis for Aunt Abby.

COME ON ADMIT IT — WE ALL LOVE A SHOW TUNE

JUNIE.
THE PLOT IS NOT ADVANCIN'

WILLIAM.
BUT SO WHAT? AT LEAST WE'RE DANCIN'

BOTH.
TO A SHOW TUNE FROM OLD BROADWAY!

(ABBY enters.)

> **ABBY**. Don't worry. I'm back! And in a stunning new gown.
> **SPOKEN STAGE DIRECTION.** The landlord enters.
> **ABBY.** Why hello there, Mr. Jitters.
> **MR. JITTERS.** You're looking well, Abby. I can tell, Abby.
> **ABBY.** Well, you know what I always say — Life could be so
> sensational if we'd all just put a little more mascara on.
> **MR. JITTERS.** Mascara? Hrummph! *(Seeing JUNIE.)* Wait
> a minute! You're that young tenant of mine who's behind on her
> rent. You must pay the rent!
> **JUNIE.** *(Exits, with WILLIAM following.)* Waaaaaaaahhhhh!
> **MR. JITTERS.** *(Angrily)* Abby! What kind of party is this?
> Where are the hors d'oeuvres?
> · **ABBY.** Where's that boy with the bagel?
> **SPOKEN STAGE DIRECTION.** Abby steps into her person-
> al haze.

ABBY.
DID I PUT OUT ENOUGH?
DID I GIVE ALL I COULD?
WE HAD CAVIAR AND BLINIS,
CRUDITES AND FRIED ZUCCHINIS
AND THOSE LITTLE COCKTAIL WEENIES – THOSE ARE
    GOOD!

DID I PUT OUT ENOUGH?
QUICK – BREAK OUT THE CHAMPAGNE!
TAKE THE TIME TO SMELL THE ROSES
LIVE IT UP AND THUMB YOUR NOSES
BEFORE LIFE GOES DOWN THE DRAIN
YES, IT'S MORE THAN ENOUGH WHEN YOU JUST ENTER-
     TAIN!

SPOKEN STAGE DIRECTION. Mr. Jitters enters in full drag, wearing a red gown and a huge feathered headdress.

ABBY. Why jumpin' Jehovah, you're just one of the girls!

MR. JITTERS. I am what I am! I took your advice and put a little mascara on. I feel so good, I want to spread it around. The rent is free!

WILLIAM. In that case, I'll pay the rent!

JUNIE. Thank you Abby! That was so helpful!

CHORUS.
THANK GOD YOU'RE HERE ABBY
YOU'RE OUR DEAR ABBY
YOUR HEART IS MADE OF PURE GOLD LAMÉ
TALK IS CHEAP AS DIRT, BUT STILL Y'KNOW
YOUR 'TWO CENTS' IS WORTH A MILLION, OH
ABBY, DEAR ABBY, DON'T EVER GO AWAY!

WE WANT YOU HERE *(We want you here!)* ABBY
WE'RE SINCERE *(We're sincere!)* ABBY!
YOUR TLC IS AOK *('Cause you're strictly SRO from A to Z)*
WOW, IT MUST BE GREAT TO BE YOU, SO
STAY RIGHT HERE WHERE WE CAN SEE YOU OH
ABBY, DEAR ABBY, DON'T EVER GO AWAY!

ABBY. Well, my work here is done. So long, dearies.

SPOKEN STAGE DIRECTION. Abby leaves aboard the "Happiness Express".

CHORUS.
OH PLEASE DON'T GO ABBY

DON'T YOU KNOW ABBY
WE'LL FALL APART IF YOU GO AWAY
WE DON'T HAVE A SHRED OF PRIDE OURSELVES
WHEN YOU'RE GONE WE'RE JUST BESIDE OURSELVES
WE COULD NEVER FILL THE BILL OURSELVES
IF YOU GO WE'LL HAVE TO KILL OURSELVES...

SPOKEN STAGE DIRECTION. Dance Break. *(Dance Break.)* Abby returns after her fortieth and final costume change of the show!

CHORUS.
WE'RE QUEER FOR DEAR ABBY!
IS THAT CLEAR ABBY?
DON'T EVER GO AWAY!

SPOKEN STAGE DIRECTION. The audience, led by gay men, rises to their feet.

CHORUS.
ABBY, ABBY, ABBY, AAAAAAH!

(Blackout)

END ACT I

ACT II

Scene: *Aspects of Junita*
In the Style of Andrew Lloyd Webber

(BILL enters, a la Che.)

BILL.
COME SEE THE SPECTACLE
COME SEE THE SHOW
A GIRL WITH AMBITION –
HOW FAR CAN SHE GO?

HER STORY'S ORIGINAL
BUT IS IT, BY CHANCE
A REALLY USEFUL PRODUCTION
OR THE OLD SONG AND DANCE?

(JUNITA enters.)

CHORUS. *(Chanting to her, adoringly.)*
JUNITA, JUNITA

PHANTOM JITTER.
YOU MUST PAY YOUR RENT

CHORUS.
PAY YOUR RENT!
PAY YOUR RENT!
PAY YOUR RENT!
PAY YOUR RENT!

JUNITA.
STAND BACK, MR. LANDLORD

I'VE TOLD YOU A MILLION TIMES
I'LL PAY THE RENT – I'LL PAY IT SOON
BUT EVERY MONTH IT'S THE SAME OLD TUNE

WELL, I'VE HEARD THAT SONG BEFORE.
I CAN'T STAND IT ANYMORE
I'LL START WHINING SOME TRITE PLATITUDE
THAT'S SHORT ON CONTENT, BUT LONG ON ATTITUDE

I'VE HEARD THAT SONG BEFORE.

BILL. *(To audience.)*
YOU'LL HEAR IT EVEN MORE...

JUNITA.
I'VE HEARD THAT SONG BEFORE.

BILL.
I'VE HEARD THAT SONG BEFORE.
YOU USED TO BE ROCK STAR
WHEN PRETENSION SOUNDED NEW
NOW LOOK WHAT YOU'VE COME TO
YOU'RE ALL WASHED UP AND SUNG THROUGH

SPOKEN STAGE DIRECTION. The landlord is revealed as none other than Sir Phantom Jitter, mysterious opera impresario, dressed in a cape and mask.

PHANTOM JITTER.
I WANT YOU TO SING FOR ME.
YOU HAVE THE VOICE OF AN ANGEL.

JUNITA. Who, me?

PHANTOM JITTER.
A WHINY, SELF-ABSORBED ANGEL.

JUNITA.
BUT I CAN'T PAY MY RENT.

PHANTOM JITTER.
I'LL FOREGO YOUR RENT IF YOU WILL SING. SOMETHING
I WROTE MYSELF.

    JUNITA. You wrote it yourself?
    PHANTOM JITTER. Do you know opera?
    JUNITA. No.
    PHANTOM JITTER. Yes, I wrote it myself.
SING A SONG THAT'S BEAUTIFUL AND NEW.
A SONG BY ME
THAT I WROTE FOR YOU.
I SWEAR IT'S TRUE.
SO SING A SONG WITH A BRAND NEW MELODY
AND BRAND NEW HARMONY,
THAT I MADE UP MYSELF IN EARLY 1987.
IT MIGHT SOUND JUST A TEENY
LIKE SOMETHING BY PUCCINI,
BUT NO, IT'S ALL BRAND NEW.
IN FACT, SO NEW THAT WHO WOULD SUE?
IT'S JUST A CASE OF DEJA VU.
IT'S NEW! IT'S NEW!

    JUNITA.
ALL I KNOW IS ROCK OPERA
I'M NOT QUITE UP TO PAR.

    PHANTOM JITTER.
THIS IS ONLY MOCK OPERA
YOU SHALL BE MY STAR.

    JUNITA.
NO, I WON'T! I WILL NEVER SING FOR THE MIDDLE
CLASSES! MY FATHER WAS MIDDLE CLASS. AND I HATED
HIM AND HE HATED ME! I ONLY LIKE THE LOWER CLASSES
AND THE UPPER CLASSES. SCREW THE MIDDLE CLASSES
AND THEIR SO-CALLED MORALITY!

SPOKEN STAGE DIRECTION. Junita storms out. The Chorus enters on roller skates.

CHORUS.
GO, GO, GO, GO JUNITA, GO!
RUN, RUN, RUN, RUN, JUNITA, RUN!
ANGELICAL JUNITA,
TIRED AND SPENT
ANGELICAL JUNITA
CAN'T PAY HER RENT
GO, GO, GO, GO JUNITA, GO!
RUN, RUN, RUN, RUN, JUNITA, RUN!

THE LANDLORD MADE AN OFFER
SHE TURNED IT DOWN
ANGELICAL JUNITA HAS A JELLICLE FROWN
GO, GO, GO, GO JUNITA
GO, JUNEYETA
GO, JUNITA, GO!

SPOKEN STAGE DIRECTION. The set changes to her boyfriend Bill's apartment. The audience applauds the set change.

JUNITA.
BILL, I'M IN TROUBLE.

BILL.
NOW WHAT?

JUNITA.
I CAN'T PAY MY RENT. I NEED YOUR HELP.

BILL.
JUNITA, I'M CONFUSED ABOUT OUR RELATIONSHIP.

JUNITA.
ME TOO. I'M TIRED OF HAVING TO SING EVERYTHING. CAN'T WE JUST TALK?

BILL.
THIS WRETCHED RECITATIVE.

JUNITA.
WHAT?

BILL.
FORGET IT.

BEHIND THE 8-BALL,
IN SEVENTH HEAVEN
DRESSED TO THE NINES,
WITH 5 O'CLOCK SHADOW

JUNITA.
I DON'T UNDERSTAND A THING YOU SAY
WE NEVER TALK ANYMORE.

BILL.
FIRST COME, FIRST SERVED

JUNITA.
PLAYIN' SECOND FIDDLE

BILL.
GETTIN' THE THIRD DEGREE,

JUNITA.
WHAT'S IT ALL FOR?

BOTH.
I DON'T UNDERSTAND A THING YOU SAY
WE NEVER TALK ANYMORE.

WE NEVER TALK
WE NEVER TALK
WE NEVER TALK
WE NEVER TALK

WE NEVER TALK
WE NEVER TALK
WE NEVER TALK
WE NEVER TALK

WE NEVER TALK ANYMORE.
WE NEVER TALK ANYMORE.

BILL.
JUNITA, I NEED TIME TO THINK. YOU SHOULD TRY TO
SOLVE YOUR OWN PROBLEMS. PAY YOUR OWN RENT.

JUNITA.
I'VE HEARD THAT SONG BEFORE
I'LL RUN RIGHT OUT THE DOOR!

SPOKEN STAGE DIRECTION. Junita runs out and talks to
herself – just another nutcase in another hall.

JUNITA.
IT'S SO UNFAIR THAT I SHOULD HAVE TO PAY MY RENT
LIKE EVERYBODY ELSE. DON'T THEY KNOW WHO I AM?

CHORUS.
A SENSE OF ENTITLEMENT
SENSE OF ENTITLEMENT
JUNITA HAS A VERY STRONG
SENSE OF ENTITLEMENT

SHE DOESN'T HAVE DEPTH
SHE DOESN'T HAVE WIT
GETS BY ON REPUTATION
THOUGH SHE'S REALLY A TWIT.

JUNITA.
PLENTY OF PEOPLE AROUND STILL ADORE ME
I CAN MAKE THE LANDLORD PAY MY RENT FOR ME

SPOKEN STAGE DIRECTION. Scene change. The audience applauds out of habit.

JUNITA.
CAN YOU HELP ME?

PHANTOM JITTER.
COME IN, MY DEAR. I'VE BEEN WAITING FOR YOU.
YOU SHALL BE MY STAR.

JUNITA.
I DON'T WANT TO BE A STAR!

PHANTOM JITTER.
THEN YOU MUST PAY YOUR RENT!

JUNITA.
I WANT TO BE A SUPER-STAR!

PHANTOM JITTER.
AH! LIKE THE GREAT JESUS CHRIST! I'LL DO FOR YOU
WHAT I DID FOR HIM. FIRST, WE RELEASE THE ALBUM,
THEN COME UP WITH A LIVE SHOW!

YOU SHALL BE MY STAR!

(ABIGAIL enters on staircase.)

ABIGAIL VON SCHTARR.
DID SOMEONE SAY STAR?

SPOKEN STAGE DIRECTION. Abigail Von Schtarr enters
from the top of the staircase.

JUNITA.
WHO'S THAT?

ABIGAIL VON SCHTARR.
PHANTOM JITTER, TELL HER WHO I AM.

PHANTOM JITTER.
MADAME IS THE GREATEST STAR WHO EVER LIVED.

JUNITA.
OH, MISS VON SCHTARR, I WANT TO BE LIKE YOU.
CAN I MAKE A COMEBACK? TELL ME WHAT TO DO.

ABIGAIL VON SCHTARR.
WELL, YOU MIGHT NEED A DRINK OR A PILL NOW
STILL THE STANDING OVATIONS WON'T STOP.
AND WHO CARES IF YOU'RE OVER THE HILL NOW?
AS LONG AS YOU'RE OVER THE TOP.

YOUR CAREER WILL TAKE OFF LIKE A NOVA
AND YOU'LL NEVER BE STUCK IN A FLOP
DO THE SAME OLD SHTICK OVER AND OVER —
AS LONG AS IT'S OVER THE TOP.

BE MORE SELF-INDULGENT
THAN YOU EVER THOUGHT YOU COULD
KEEP IT LOUD THEN ADD MORE REVERB
PEOPLE THINK IT'S GOOD. AHHHHHHHHH…

AND YOUR NAME WILL STAY OVER THE TITLE —
AS LONG AS YOU'RE OVER THE TOP.

JUNITA.
THANK YOU MISS VON SCHTARR. THAT WAS SO HELP-
FUL.

(ABIGAIL exits. BILL enters.)

BILL.
I FOLLOWED YOU HERE
YOU CAN'T DISAPPEAR
I WON'T LET YOU FALL FOR HIS SEDUCTION

PHANTOM JITTER.
YOU'RE NOTHING BUT TRASH

I CAN GIVE HER PANACHE
'CAUSE EVERYTHING I DO'S A BIG PRODUCTION

BILL.
JUNITA, IS THIS TRUE?

JUNITA.
HE SAYS HE CAN MAKE ME A STAR

BILL.
DON'T YOU KNOW? – YOU ALREADY ARE!

Junita, we have to talk. Yes, talk! I've come to tell you, I'll pay the rent!

PHANTOM JITTER.
SHE WILL BE MY NEW STAR!

BILL.
(Gasps.) STAND BACK, MY JUNITA
WATCH OUT FOR THAT CHANDELIER
IT'S FALLING DOWN AND YOU'LL BE HIT

JUNITA.
YOU THINK I'D FALL FOR THAT OLD BIT?
WELL, I'VE HEARD THAT SONG BEF…*YAHHHHH!*

(JUNITA falls.)

SPOKEN STAGE DIRECTION. Abigail enters holding wire clippers.

ABIGAIL VON SCHTARR.
THERE'S ONLY ROOM FOR ONE DIVA IN THIS TOWN!

BILL.
LOOK WHAT YOU'VE DONE!
FIEND! WHO ARE YOU?

SPOKEN STAGE DIRECTION. He pulls off the mask in anger, revealing Phantom Jitter's hideous face — with whiskers, striped fur and pointy ears.

BILL. My God! You're a..a…cat! A cat of many colors!

PHANTOM JITTER.
I WAS BORN LIKE THIS — DEFORMED AND SCARRED
MY LIFE HAS BEEN VERY HARD
FRISKIES IN THE MORNING, HAIR BALL AFTER LUNCH
DOGS CHASIN' AFTER ME
BUT NOW ALL I DO IS SLEEP ALL DAY
'CAUSE I WAS NEUTERED AT THE AGE OF THREE

I'm sorry, Junita.

JUNITA. *(Weary of drama.)* Whatever.

BILL.
THAT WAS THE SPECTACLE
THAT WAS THE SHOW
JUNITA IS DEAD NOW
SO WHAT DO YOU KNOW.

CHORUS.
HEY SANNA, HO SANNA, ADIOS AMIGA.

SPOKEN STAGE DIRECTION. Junita, not quite dead yet, manages to sing her dying farewell.

JUNITA.
DID I HAVE GENIUS? NEVER.
DID I HAVE GREATNESS? NEVER.
BUT WAS I A COMMERCIAL SUCCESS?
YES — NOW AND FOREVER!

SPOKEN STAGE DIRECTION. She ascends into the stratosphere on the rising chandelier. The audience applauds the smoke machine.

(Blackout.)

Scene: *Speakeasy*
In the Style of Kander and Ebb

SPOKEN STAGE DIRECTION. Lights up in a Cabaret in Chicago. It's the thirties — Prohibition. Speakeasy.

JÜTTER.
THE WORLD CAN GO TO BLAZES
WHO CARES? IT DOESN'T FAZE US
WE'VE GOT BOOZE
AND SONGS THAT USE
A LOT OF FOREIGN PHRASES

HOLA, ALOHA, HELLO

GIRLS.
SHHHH

JÜTTER.
WE'RE IN A SPEAKEASY
BYE-BYE, TA-TA, CHEERIO

GIRLS.
SHHHH

JÜTTER.
SPEAKEASY
HASTA LA VISTA AND ERIN GO BRAGH
ACHOO AND GESUNDHEIT
AND QUE SERA, SERA...JAH!
HOLA, ALOHA, HELLO

GIRLS.
SHHHH

JÜTTER.
WE'RE IN A SPEAKEASY
DRINK YOUR WINE 'CAUSE LIFE'S A CABERNET
YOU MIGHT GET A DRINKY, YOU MIGHT GET A SMOKEY

AND IF YOU'RE KINDA KINKY, IT MIGHT BE OKEY-DOKEY
AT THE SPEAKEASY
IT'S HARD TO SAY.

Here at the Speakeasy, we speak many different languages. But the favorite is Pig-Latin. To fool the police, Jah? Sprechen zie Eutche-Day? Parlez-vous Rancais-Fay? Et tu Brute? Ha, ha, ha, ha. That was real Latin! Ha, ha, ha, ha. Now, bring on the slutty dancing girls!

GIRLS.
HOLA, ALOHA, HELLO

JÜTTER.
LIFE IS LIKE A LITTLE SHOW

GIRLS.
BYE-BYE, ADIO, ADIEU

JÜTTER.
LIFE IS LIKE A WEIRD REVUE
YOU MIGHT SNORT A LITTLE COKIE OR SIP A LITTLE
    SAKE
WITH A SPOOKY OLD KABUKI AND HIS GOOKY SUKIYAKI
    AT THE SPEAKEASY
IT'S HARD TO SAY.

GIRLS.
SHHHH...

(They exit.)

JÜTTER. So, life is good? Forget it! In here, life is disappointing. You cannot pay your rent. Like one of our own Speakeasy girls, Guny.

JUNY.
THAT'S JUNY WITH A "J"

NOT GUNY WITH A "G"
'CAUSE JUNY WITH A "J"
GOES "DGE" NOT "GUH"
THAT'S JUNY WITH A "J"
NOT GUNY WITH A "G"
'CAUSE JUNY WITH A "J"
GOES "DGE"

(JÜTTER knocks three times.)

    JUNY. Who is it?
    JÜTTER. Zah landlord!
    JUNY. The landlord!?
    JÜTTER. Pay the rent
    JUNY. I can't. Bye-bye!
    JÜTTER. Guny, pay zah rent!

    JUNY.
THAT'S JUNY WITH A "J"
NOT GUNY WITH A "G"
'CAUSE JUNY WITH A "J"
GOES "DGE"

    SLUTTY CHORUS GIRL. Juny goes to visit her boyfriend
Villy in a prison full of singing and dancing inmates.
    JUNY. Oh, Villy. I'm in a real fix. It seems I can't pay my rent.
Villy, I need your help.
    · **VILLY.** I'm no help to you. I've changed here in jail. Leave me
here with my fantasies and my coloring books.

SEE THE GUARD BY THE DOOR?
COLOR HIM BLUE
SEE THE GIRL WHO'S SO MAD?
COLOR HER RED
SEE THE GUY WITH THE GRAY HAT AND COAT?
COLOR HIM…GRAY
SEE THE BOYFRIEND WHO WON'T PAY THE RENT?
COLOR ME GAY

JUNY. Gay? But we were lovers!

VILLY. Yeah, well, things are different nowadays. Go back to the Speakeasy; if you can make it there, you'll make it anywhere. Good-bye, Luny.

JUNY.
IT'S JUNY WITH A "J"
NOT LUNY WITH AN "L"
'CAUSE JUNY WITH A "J"
GOES "DGE" NOT "UHLL".
IT'S JUNY WITH A "J"
NOT LUNY WITH AN "L"
'CAUSE JUNY WITH A "J"
GOES "DGE".

Aw, forget it.

JÜTTER. Ladies und Gentleman, Guys und Gals, Spidermen und Spiderwomen. Vhat happens to young girls who don't pay their rent?

CHORUS.
(Solos, a la "Cellblock Tango")
DRIP
SQUEAK
MINNELLI
SCREWED

DRIP
SQUEAK
MINNELLI
SCREWED

(Unison)
I NEVER PAID, I NEVER PAID NO RENT
I NEVER PAID, NO, NO NOT ONE RED CENT
TOO BAD I STIFFED HIM
IT MIGHT'A MIFFED HIM BUT I
JUST DON'T PAY!

CHORUS PERSON. So, I'm tryin' to sleep in my apartment. And all I can hear is "drip, drip, drip". That faucet's been drippin' since the day I moved in. So, I told the landlord, "Look, I ain't payin' no rent until you fix that DRIP"...

ANOTHER CHORUS PERSON. I used to have this girlfriend known as Elsie. We used to share four sordid rooms in uh, you know, the Flatiron District. Well. there was this one floorboard that used to squeak so loud. And I told that landlord, "If I hear one more SQUEAK...

FOREIGN SPEAKING CHORUS PERSON. Kinooschjka mit ooben zee mischka wobblin. Za bolschka wobbling. Iskcha wobble, wobblleshschka! Mit ikshken za landlorda "No More MINELLI!"

CHORUS.
I NEVER PAID, I NEVER PAID NO RENT
I NEVER PAID, THAT MONEY'S ALL BEEN SPENT
KEEP MY DEPOSIT
CLEAN OUT MY CLOSET
'CAUSE I JUST DON'T PAY!

(Rhythmic knocking –)

CHORUS. Who is it?
JÜTTER. Zah landlord!
CHORUS. The landlord? We just don't pay!
JÜTTER. I'm SCREWED!

CHORUS.
I NEVER PAID, I NEVER PAID NO RENT
I NEVER PAID, I AIN'T NO RESIDENT
THEY MIGHT HARANGUE YOU,
THEY'LL NEVER HANG YOU IF YOU
JUST DON'T PAY

I NEVER PAID, I NEVER PAID NO RENT
I NEVER PAID, I AIN'T NO RESIDENT

THEY MIGHT HARANGUE YOU,
THEY'LL NEVER HANG YOU IF YOU
JUST DON'T PAY

JÜTTER. Meine damen und airheads, zah speakeasy iss proud
to present: Schloony!

JUNY.
THAT'S JUNY WITH A "J"
NOT SCHLUNY WITH A "SCHL"
'CAUSE JUNY WITH A J GOES
"DGE" NOT "SCHL"

JÜTTER. Zah rent iss due!
JUNY. I can't pay!
JÜTTER. Ladies und Germans, who can tell her what to do?
Direct from Munich, Fraulein Abby! Vhat vould you do?

FRAULEIN ABBY.
SELL YOUR BODY
DON'T COMPLAIN
SLIP 'EM A MICKIE
THEN THROW 'EM A QUICKIE
AUF WIEDERSEHEN!
TAKE IT FROM ME,
IT'S A WALK IN THE PARK
FIND YOURSELF AN EASY MARK.

EAGER MEN WILL PAY YOUR PRICE
WHEN YOU'RE HOT, THEY SPOT IT
IT'S VERY SPECIAL MERCHANDISE
YOU SELL IT – YOU STILL GOT IT!

Jah, ven ve first moved to Chicago, ve vere so poor, mein husband
sent me out to sell myself on the street. I vas gone for two hours.
When I came back, he said, "Vell? How much did you make?" I
said, "50 dollars und 10 cents". He said, "10 cents? Who gave you
10 cents?" And I told him, "They all did!"

WHY GO HUNGRY
THIN AND PALE
WHISPER A COY LINE
THEN MOVE OVER FRAULEIN
YOU'VE MADE A SALE!
NO ONE'S A SAINT
WHO ARE YOU? JOAN OF ARC?
FIND YOURSELF AN EASY MARK.

JÜTTER. Thank you, Fraulein Abby. That was so helpful.

JUNY. *(Over vamp.)* You wanna know somethin'? I always wanted to pay my rent, but I never could. I had me a world full of "no". But now, I'm gonna get me a world full of "maybe — this time".

AIN'T WE ALL GOT FUN?
ALL OUR SORROWS DROWNED?
THE WORLD IS A DARK AND EVIL PLACE THAT KEEPS
SPINNING ROUND AND ROUND

CHORUS.
SO, YOU THINK YOU WANT TO GO WITH YOUR BEAU
TO THE CLUB HOTSY-TOTSY
FOR A DRINK AND SOME KISSES AND HUGS?
NO, YOU'LL END UP IN A DIVE
WHERE YOUR BOYFRIEND IS QUEER FOR SOME NAZI
AND YOU'LL ALL GET ADDICTED TO DRUGS

SUPPOSE YOU'RE AT A DANCE –THERE'S A CHANCE
THAT YOU MIGHT WIN SOME MONEY
WITH SOME FUN AND ROMANCE INTERMIXED
YOU'RE REALLY IN A DUMP IN THE DEPTHS
OF A REALLY BAD DEPRESSION
AND THE MARATHON IS FIXED.

JUNY.
TAKE YOUR HOPES AND DREAMS
CRUSH THEM IN THE GROUND
THE WORLD IS A DARK AND EVIL PLACE THAT KEEPS

SPINNING ROUND AND ROUND.

JÜTTER. Und now an act of desperation!

JUNY. I'll pay the rent like this: Take my body and use it in a perfectly marvelous way

JÜTTER. I'm not interested. You are a dirty girl!

FRAULEIN ABBY. Take mein body – please!

JÜTTER. It's clearly been taken already. Many times, no?

VILLY. Wait! I'll pay the rent! Take *my* body!

JÜTTER. Jah, iss good! Zah rent iss paid! Ha, ha, ha, ha, ha.

ALL.
LIFE'S A CRUEL CHARADE
THAT'S WHAT I HAVE FOUND
THE WORLD IS A DARK AND EVIL PLACE THAT KEEPS
SPINNING ROUND AND ROUND.

JÜTTER.
BYE-BYE
GOOD-BYE NOW
BYE-BYE!

(Blackout.)

Scene: *FINALE*

(Lights come up once more for the finale, sung as solos, duets, or other vocal combination, as needed.)

CAST.
DONE
NOW THE SHOW IS OVER SO
RUN
SCREAMING FOR THE EXIT WE'RE
DONE
NOT A MOMENT TOO SOON

IT'S OVER

DONE
FOR THEATRE COGNOSCENTI
DONE
SO WE COULD PAY THE RENT-Y
FUN
BUT NOW IT'S DONE

YOU WALK INTO A SHOW AND HOPE YOU
DON'T FALL ASLEEP WATCHING THE PLOT
YOU WALK INTO A SHOW AND FIND YOU'RE
WATCHING THE SAME PLOT A LOT

SO MANY POINTS OF VIEW, THOUGH
COULDN'T THEY WRITE A NEW SHOW?
PROBABLY NOT,
IT'S ALL BEEN DONE

(Repeat in two groups, overlapping.)

DONE
NOW THE SHOW IS OVER SO
RUN
SCREAMING FOR THE EXIT WE'RE
DONE
NOT A MOMENT TOO SOON

IT'S OVER
DONE
FOR THEATRE COGNOSCENTI
DONE
SO WE COULD PAY THE RENT-Y
FUN
BUT NOW IT'S DONE

YOU WALK INTO A SHOW AND HOPE YOU
DON'T FALL ASLEEP WATCHING THE PLOT
YOU WALK INTO A SHOW AND FIND YOU'RE
WATCHING THE SAME PLOT A LOT

SO MANY POINTS OF VIEW, THOUGH
COULDN'T THEY WRITE A NEW SHOW?
PROBABLY NOT,
IT'S ALL BEEN DONE
(In unison.)

DONE
NOTHING ELSE TO SAY SO WE'RE
DONE
YET WE KEEP ON SINGING
"WE'RE DONE"
LIKE YOU DON'T UNDERSTAND

YOU SEE IT'S
OVER
WHY ARE YOU STILL SITTING THERE?
OVER
ANOTHER WORD FOR OVER IS
DONE
IT'S OVER
DONE!

CURTAIN

OTHER TITLES AVAILABLE FROM SAMUEL FRENCH

THE ALTOS

David Landau
Music & Lyrics by Nikki Stern

4m, 3f / Full Length / Musical Comedy / Interior

Like 'The Sopranos', only lower!

An Interactive Musical Comedy Mystery Spoof of the famous HBO series. Meet the family that inspired it all, the Altos. It's Tony's funeral (Or is it?) and his wife Toffee has invited you to the wake. Chris wants you should check your weapons at the door (and if you don't have any, he's got extras!) Uncle Senior has a rigged dice game going and Tony's Ma is - well just nuts. Tony's shrink Dr. Malaise is giving free analysis and the Father isn't sure what he is doing! But one thing is for sure, almost no one seems sad that Tony is gone and they certainly done seem happy once he's discovered alive. Be prepared to dodge bullets, laugh at the songs and see if you can't figure out who put a contract out on Tony!